HUSTLER IN THE MAFIA

SOPHIA RAZ

This is a work of fiction. Names, characters, places, and incidents either are the product of the author's imagination or are used fictitiously. Any resemblance to actual persons, living or dead, events, or locales is entirely coincidental.

First edition January 2025

Cover design - Getcovers
Beta readers – Eleanor Tevendale, Raluca.M.Matara, Shaunie Schoonejans, Annalisa Dawn & Emma Williams.
Editors – Amy Scott & Emma Williams from Scott Editorial

ISBN 978-9-4649-4914-8 (ebook)
ISBN 978-9-4649-4915-5 (paperback)

www.sophiaraz.com

To all the girls who don't want their future defined by where they were born. You are more than the crib that held you.

ALSO BY SOPHIA RAZ

From my heart to yours: Thank you so much for taking the time to read my book baby.
Princess of the Mafia is the second book of The Shadows of the Cosa Nostra Chronicles. They don't have to be read in order, but it's a much better experience to do so since they are interconnected characters.

The Shadows of Cosa Nostra Chronicles:

Nanny to the Mafia:
Book 01 - Antonio and Divya's story
Princess of the Mafia:
Book 02 - Lorenzo and Daria's story
Runaway in the Mafia:
Book 03 - Vitale and Ahana's story
Book 04 - Pre-order now

The Shadows of Cosa Nostra Chronicles:

Hustler in the Mafia:
Book 01.5 - Marco and Florina's story

CONTENTS

Hustler in the Mafia
Tropes and trigger warnings

To my readers:

Hustler in the Mafia is the novella from The Shadows of Cosa Nostra Chronicles. This takes place between books 01 and 02. The series contains interconnected characters, and each book can be read as a standalone. This is a Mafia romance and can therefore contain content and situations that could be triggering for some readers. This book also has explicit sexual content and is intended for readers 18+

Featuring the following tropes:

Mafia romance, enemies to lovers, he falls first, age gap, instalust, forced proximity, hero, obsessive MMC, Badass FMC, Homeless FMC and hero MMC.

Trigger warnings:

Abused FMC, homelessness, parental death (off the page), talk of rape (not by MMC), talk of prostitution, gore, morally grey, explicit sex scenes, killing, blood, guns, abusive parent, violence, murder & death, self sabotage and light degradation.

Disclaimer:

- Rromani - Is another modern term accepted to refer to Romani people. They are known by a variety of names, mostly as Gypsies, Roma, Tsinganoi, Bohémiens,... Rromani is a correct way of referring to them. Some other names such as Gypsies can bring insult to them.

- The MMC calls the FMC his little coconut. Even though the correct term for this in Italian is *la mia piccola noce di cocco*. In this book, the author has taken the liberty of changing it to *la mia piccola cocco* therefore choosing the cuteness of how it will sound above the accurate use of the language.

- **Please note:** This book is written in British English.

PROLOGUE

PALERMO, SICILY, ITALY

VALTH

Power was his drug. Strength, an addiction that thrummed in his veins. The source that would pulse his heart with both was just beyond reach. For days, he had chased her. From Tirane to Durres and right throughout fucking Italy to Corleone. He was stronger. He was faster, and he was for sure smarter. Only thing she had was luck on her side. He should have caught her and fucked her out of her brains already in Tirane. Instead, the filthy bitch kept slipping past him like sand seeping through his fingers.

But the time to run had passed. Finally, he was close. He could smell her trail. Fear and hunger left behind by her slippery feet, thumping through the depths of the thick forest. If she had been smart, she would have only been fucked and broken. But now she had pissed him off. Made him feel weak when he was anything but that. Worse. She had made him feel stupid. Always having the upper hand. A mere woman. A whore. Was she so stupid not to know that it was only luck on her side that had kept her out of reach?

Even that had run out since she had trapped herself in the thick of this forest. No one around to protect her. No lone building constructions to hide in or dark alleys to creep into shadows. Nah. Even the God she undoubtedly prayed to was letting go. Opening the drain to let the filth that she was flush out. Because the light was thinning out and the sun was going to bed. The only thing that remained was the rush of rustling leaves and the cold wind carrying the harsh gasps of her painful breaths.

You are going down, stupid bitch.

He moved, slow and steady, to her panicked and skidding feet. The bitch had a shit load of luck with her. He'd give her that. She had gotten to the bus faster, the ferry even faster, but ultimately, he was the master planner in this. Not her.

Just like in a marathon, when you start fast, you run out of steam before the finish line. What was that saying again? Something about a hare and a tortoise. Only he was the fucking panther here.

Because now, finally, he could see her, zipping between the trees, breath wheezing past, shoulders hunched, and arms clutching her midriff.

The thrill of almost catching her burst through his body, and a hearty laugh spilled out of his lips. Well, it wasn't an accident. He wanted her to know, to hear, that he was almost upon her.

Her head snapped to him, just like he had wanted. Her sunken eyes skidded to his own. What she saw there must have conveyed his intentions because her eyes lost the little life they had left, and she sunk to her knees with a gasp.

That's right, my filthy whore. I was only going to fuck your three holes a hundred times and leave you to die. But now I will do that and use my favourite knife to carve your body and watch the birds fly as you breathe your last breath.

He slowed his pace. Good things in life had to be relished. His heavy booted feet stomped down on the fallen leaves, marking the progress of the predator in him coming close to his prey. Didn't she look like a heavenly one, too.

His hands tingled with anticipation. His cock jerked, ready for action.

Yes, my little boy, you are going to get a lot of action.

He was a mere five feet away. Close enough to smell the fear and see the sweat dripping down her neck as she hunched on the ground. Her gasps filled the air and brought a thrill to his bones.

A twig snapped, and he froze. His eyes shot to his feet and then to her. He hadn't moved, and neither had she.

Another snap and the sound of heavy footsteps approaching.

Both of their eyes snapped in unison to find the view beyond the thick trees, still too warm to shed all of their leaves.

Fucking hell.

There was a house looming ahead. Well, not a house, a fucking mansion.

Not again.

"Mos guxo, kurvë," he growled and sprang to latch onto her shoulder, but it was already too late.

A spark lit her eyes, and with a kick of her feet, she sprinted through the forest with new energy and left him behind. Again.

CHAPTER ONE

FLORINA

F*uck!* That was close. Pulse drumming in my ears, trees whizzing past my vision, and nausea crawling up my throat.

Thud thud.

My pounding feet on rough earth. A tree trunk punched my view, and a second later, I smacked into it. *Goddammit.* I crawled through the dirt and jerked up again. I didn't have time to nurse a fucking headache. I was almost there and swiftly dared to look behind me. He was out of my vision. Thank you, God.

My chest ached and burned like the hot engine of an old car, ready to throttle down. I couldn't go on. My pace slowed. I wanted to keel over and die. Giving up would be so easy. Here on the sodden mud path leading from the forest to the villa in front. But not my damn mind. It dragged my body along like a heavy anchor, clattering and clamming with wheezing breath.

I wish I could say this was the closest I'd come to facing death. My life wasn't a bed of thorns but rather one with sharp-edged nails. The innumerable times that Tata's boot-clad foot latched on to my body like I was his favourite punchbag made this look like a fucking joke. At least with Tata, he might have gone to the effort to bury my body. He and Mama might have even had a funeral. With booze and hookers, but still, they would have given a show. Tata would have invited his drinking buddies, and Mama would have asked her pimp and her clients to come mourn with her. They probably would have had an orgy or something to celebrate my death.

But I bet the nasty animal with bad breath you could smell a mile off wouldn't have done that. I should have known. I was a lot of things. A thief, a liar, the worst daughter on the planet, and unworthy of anything good in my life. But I wasn't an idiot. Still, it was like the lack of food was making the small amount of wisdom in my brain drain out. I should have fucking known that this particular Albanian couldn't be played with.

My mama had big plans for me. She called me beautiful. She envisioned the money I would bring her. But turned out I was her biggest mistake. Because this beauty came with a loud mouth and an insane kick. Any man who reached his grubby hands for my pussy got blue balls delivered like a fucking phantom in a black box. They never saw it coming. Not a single one of them. But still, beggars couldn't be choosers. My game was simple. I did what I needed to do to survive. Some people used their brains to bring in the money. Some their hands. I used my body. Every time I dropped to my knees, it shone a light on my sorry existence. I'd done it too many times to keep count but too little to learn to enjoy it. Every time a man shoved his dick into my mouth, it felt like the slither of a venomous snake. Every time a man groped my body, it felt like red ants crawling on my skin. But there came a time when the desire for food or the comfort of a trouble-free night far outweighed any morals I would want to hang on to except one. I never gave them my body.

But, of course, the knucklehead wanted what he couldn't have. The moment his beefy hand snuck out and fisted my jaw, I knew he was going to be bad news. But it was already too late. The alley was dark, the night cold, and, in all honesty, who would even want to listen to the screams of a runaway girl? Not even my own Rromani community would come out to help when I'd dumped them at the first opportunity four years ago.

So, I used another one of my talents. I played along with him, I hummed and moaned and encouraged him and let his sweat-soaked hands plaster me with bruises until he let his guard down and dropped his pants on the floor. Then, I did what any good girl would do. I wrenched his arm, kicked him in the balls, and ran for my life. That kick worked every single time. Oh, I also took his glittery watch off his wrist when I had my foot on his balls.

That was a tad too much, maybe. I wasn't sure if it was that or his blue balls that made him follow me across Albania and all throughout Italy. Ditching countries wasn't enough to keep him off. He was like a fucking leach, and he just wouldn't let go. Three days of always being a breath away from him. I had it coming when I left him behind at a bus halt or a ferry stop. His cold eyes pinned to my triumphant ones. I should have known. My luck was running out. Even faster than that was the money that was dwindling, with only a thin lining to show in my drawstring pouch and the size of a pinkie hole at the edge of it.

Was it the heaviness of the weightless pouch that made me make this stupid decision to come back to this place? I could argue it was a mere coincidence. But last night, when I had hidden in an abandoned factory, I had made use of it to snatch a small plier to cut open the metal fencing around this property. The villa loomed larger than life as I neared it. It spread majestically over the land, sucking it up with ivory walls and wooden windows. It was just a facade. Behind it lived men who took a life with a snap of their fingers. I couldn't tell if the gasps in my breath were my body letting go or my fear throttling up.

The last time I had been here was almost two years ago. When Antonio Capizzi found me hiding in his library, listening to his conversation with his father, I thought he'd kill me. The only good thing about that would have been that I would have died at the hands of a man who looked hot as sin. But, of course, I didn't have that luck. He chucked me out to Peppe, one of his servants, and warned me never to come back. Well... 'warned' was putting it lightly.

"If I ever see you anywhere near us again... I will deliver you as food to your family in a fucking box."

I didn't have any family. Not anymore. But when the *Consigliere* of the Mafia threatened me like that, the wise girl inside me took the advice. So I ran as fast and far as possible. I couldn't say it had all been bad. I had some good times. Travelled a bit. Took a long holiday. I thought hiding in the luggage compartment of busses and lounging around back alleys of restaurants should be called vacationing as well. I bet I saw the realness of a city more than its inhabitants.

But now the holiday was over, and I was back here. Because deep down, I knew if there was any place I could hide where that vile man wouldn't dare come further, it was near the house of the *Consigliere*. Near. I wasn't an idiot. I wasn't going inside that house and getting myself caught. I would just hang around here until the Albanian left and take off.

Besides, there was another man I needed to avoid here. Peppe. The idiot who's dick I was sucking last time to get some food. Let's just say he wasn't thrilled when his fire-breathing boss found me tucked away in his library.

My stomach cramped again, curling in on itself from the painful hollowness. Three days I'd been slinking into the shadows cast by the house. The Albanian hadn't given up. He didn't come closer, but he circled me as I circled the house. We kept at it. Both of us. Why was I always the prey in my life? For once, I wanted to be the stronger one. During the day, I stuck to the thickness of the trees, staying away from the servants and the men with angry faces, but during the night, I sneaked around to the bins outside the kitchen to find some leftovers.

Only, every time, I'd been finding more than leftovers. A cold salad on the windowsill, a lukewarm lasagne next to the bin. All untouched, with a fork right next to it like it was dished out just for me. Hunger was a weird thing. It made me hallucinate that someone was looking out for me. I swallowed the big lump in my throat. *As if.* But it didn't stop me from chucking that fork out and stuffing that lasagne in my mouth with my cold, grubby hands like my life depended on it.

Then, the night before, I had found a tiramisu just in front of the kitchen door, and I knew for sure. Someone was watching me. The heat on the back of my neck that made the hair stand out wasn't from a sudden blast of hot air, it was because someone's eyes had landed on mine. How long would it take before I had to drop to my knees?

For a nanosecond, I'd thought it was the hot *Consigliere.* Except I knew I'd already be dead if he'd found me because he looked like a man who kept his word. So it was one of his men. Was this why I could sneak around without getting caught? Someone liked me. I could almost taste the sourness of a gratitude blow job in the future.

But I was wrong again. Someone *had* liked me. There was no food around tonight. Nothing. Even the garbage was empty, like they'd determined I wasn't even worthy of their trash. Hot tears burned the back of my eyes as I clutched my stomach and crawled my way to the back door.

For once. Just once in my fucked-up life, I wanted a fucking break. If I wasn't blessed with a loving father, I should have had an angel of a mother. But no. My whore of a mother's only advice was that the cum of men would provide enough vitamins for me. Could I then just maybe have been blessed with a fresh plate of food for one day without having to jerk someone off?

The cavity in my belly ached with such emptiness that it trilled through my body. I just wanted one fucking meal. And one less Albanian in my life. If I had to choose, I would still choose the meal.

I was done. Past all this shit that life threw at me. Hunger made me courageous. Previous near-death experiences drained out of me as easily as dirty water in a sink. *Cristo!* Was I doing this? With a tremble in my hand, I latched on to the handle, pulled it down, and pushed the door open.

It was a villa, but the damn place was old. It smelled of centuries of family money, and the loud creak of the door echoed and bounced off all the colourfully pigmented fresco walls.

Just my luck. I squeezed my eyes shut and slowly counted to ten wheezing breaths. My eyes flickered open, expecting an army of men before me. Not a single man with a gun stood in sight.

Maybe today was going to be my lucky day.

With new confidence and a sweep of my feet, I stood up and scanned the kitchen that I had observed for days with my eyes glued to the windows. Warm terracotta tiles everywhere. A large, robust table extending to the dark corners swallowed the left side of the room. It wasn't enough to spark a second of my attention. To the right stood the big, ivory fridge, as shiny as an elephant's tusk, surrounded by rusty wooden cabinets. But what caught my eye was the *pièce de résistance* on top of the marble countertop, right next to the sink in front of the window. It shone brighter than a jewel and made me hotter than a fire. Had I seen that view from outside, I would have crashed through the glass. A full plate of pasta. So hot I could see the smoke whiffing off it and smell the freshness standing five meters away.

Cautiousness slipped off me and thudded to the floor like a heavy and unwanted coat. With quick steps, I paced to the corner. A smart girl would have floated above this deliciousness and pondered. *Is this too good to be true?* But a famished girl would have done exactly what I did. Skip the cutlery lying next to it and shovel a big heap into my greedy mouth.

A loud groan burst from my mouth. This must be what heaven felt like... and hell. My choked gasp split the air as a thick hand wrapped around my throat.

"What's this filth in the kitchen?" The cold threat of Peppe's voice assaulted me a second before he whipped me around to thrust his face inches from me. His nasty breath gusted up my nostrils as my own whooshed out of mine.

"What you going to do this time to get out of this fix?"

Fight. That's what I always did. I latched onto his hand, which was choking me, and dug my nails into it.

"Fucking gypsies." His grip tightened, and his other hand bruised the side of my rib as he pushed his whole body onto my pelvis, his erect dick poking into me. A sharp stab of pain shot up my back as it hit the brass cabinet knob. All I needed was the space to shove my knee into his balls.

"It better be more than a blowjob this time," he sneered as my vision coloured black around me.

Fuck! This really was the end. The force of his grip on my neck and the big lump of pasta stuck in my throat was going to be my end. They say your life passes before your eyes before you die. The thin, filthy line edging along my eyeballs must have been mine. The harsh thumps of Tata's foot, Mama's plastic moans pleasuring a client in the bed next to mine, the first and only boy I fell in love with, especially his words when I opened up to him after he took my virginity. *"Wait. You thought I'd love a filthy girl like you?"*

"Should I fuck you alive, or should I fuck you dead?" my current lifeline sneered.

Nothing had changed. Years later. It was another man and his cruel words. Only difference was my heart wasn't involved because there wasn't anything left to give.

Just like that, I decided it was enough. I had enough of this and was ready to let go. My body went limp, and the fight went out of me.

"Let her go."

The darkness sucking my energy let go. The grip around my neck released, and Peppe stepped away with a look on his face I couldn't fathom. I couldn't give a shit. With a gasp, I turned around weakly to the sink and emptied the rest of the pasta that choked up my throat.

Fuck. It burned. My throat felt like someone poured

gasoline and a spark of fire in it and jammed my mouth shut. Hot tears and snot rolled out of me as I tried to get a grip on myself. *What the hell happened?*

I whipped my tear-filled eyes around frantically, trying to find the source. Because Peppe hadn't stopped out of his own will. Or had he? My panicked gaze picked up nothing except Peppe. He stood in front of me, glaring at me like a kid who wasn't allowed to smash his least favorite toy.

"Is this how you get off?" a harsh voice rumbled from the far corner of the dining table. "Preying on fragile women?"

Fragile? I wasn't fragile. My shoulders stiffened, and my back went ramrod straight. I huffed my breath, and my mouth popped open...

"Shut the fuck up."

What? How the hell did the voice know I was about to...

"Now, come here and sit down."

Peppe shuffled his feet.

"Not you, you idiot."

He meant me? With more reluctance than Peppe, I slowly side-stepped past him and inched closer to the table. I was good at recognising voices. This didn't belong to the *Consigliere.* I was sure of it. Not his brother, either. I'd heard him. This belonged to someone else.

The dim, porcelain, bell-shaped light with the painted pink roses hung too low on top of the table to see much other than the scratched surface of the wooden top. Standing a few breaths away from the end of the table, all I could see was the dark shadow of a wide shoulder within a big frame. Not as big as the man who had chased me, but still big.

The chair next to him scraped the floor, the sound crackling in the quiet kitchen.

"Sit," he ordered, and for a girl who never took kindly to an order, I stepped forward and plonked down on the stool so fast I would have made my dead parents happy. *Had they been those kind of parents.*

"Now warm that food up," he snapped at Peppe. He didn't scream, but the harshness in his voice had the same effect. "And bring her a glass of wine." A hot drift of air fell on my lips. "Red."

The air around me shuffled with sultry awareness. So this was the man who'd been watching me. I was sure of it. A warm light flicked on right next to him, and two things became clear to me.

One, it wasn't only the two Capizzi brothers who were hot enough to burn hell.

Two, I guess I wasn't done sucking someone's dick for food. Because the look on his face told me he was anything but a saint.

CHAPTER TWO

MARCO

I saw her, and I wanted her. Her body, her words, her thoughts. The moment she stepped out of the trees, she crossed the line and stepped into my territory. And I wasn't talking about the tangible boundary wall made up of barbed wire and metal barricades lining across the Capizzi property. There was something in her that called out to my broken and malfunctioned heart. It wanted her and all the sinful sighs she would echo hereafter. Insanity sputtered in my veins like the hard throb of a pounding headache. *This woman was mine.* She was weak in her body but a fighter in her mind. Her strong will and determination shone through the grubbiness of filth and starvation like a diamond unspoiled.

For three fucking days, I had watched her. She was like a precious little bird. *Il mio passerotto.* Always twirling her head around and ready to fly off at the slightest sound. Yet her spirit shone through of an eagle hiding under the guise of a sparrow.

I couldn't really pinpoint what it was about her. Was it her fucking body? Big tits were my wet dream, and she had that and more. Or was it because she reminded me of someone I used to be? Or perhaps her strong mind? Whatever it was, it made me want to pick her up and hide her within my suit-clad body.

She was sex on a stick, even though her cheeks were hollow and her eyes sunken in. I could see what she would be like with good food for a week. *Fuck!* I could see exactly what she would look like down on her knees with those pretty pink lips wrapped around my thick cock.

She was smart, light, and flexible. None of the other men seemed to have noticed her. Which didn't bode well for my security. But she couldn't outsmart me. I'd seen her three nights ago, creeping out of her hiding place behind the trees.

My first instinct should have been to yank her by her ear and kick her cute tush back to wherever she had come from. Except I'd allowed indecision to sweep in, and I let her hang around.

Maybe it was because she reminded me of myself. Twenty-five fucking years ago, grubbing around the household garbage until Antonio caught me and yanked me off the bin by my ear. We were the same age. But I don't know what pissed me off more. Poverty, starvation, or the fact that he could kick my ass even though I was bigger. He hammered me into a puddle, took the bin, and smashed it on my head, and just when I thought it was going to be my final moment, he yanked me inside, pushed me into a shower, and shoved a warm plate of food under my nose. Before the hour was up, he had introduced me to his father as his friend. All of this before he'd even asked my name. I thought I didn't belong anywhere. Turned out, at ten years old, Antonio thought I did. As the right-hand man to the future *Consigliere* of the Mafia. He made me his family, and I him.

But it didn't stop the never-ending ache of loneliness of growing up as an orphan. Of carrying a surname that had no meaning and no link to a father. A moment of thought or a whiff of a smell if the wind blew in the wrong direction and I was right there. Sleeping in ditches and prowling in garbage bins. Just like when I saw her. The stink of old food and the ache of an empty belly drilled through my big body like a cement drill on my chest.

My master plan had been to give her food for a week and kick her out. I needed her away from the house. Antonio and his family's protection was my only priority. A little Rromani girl hiding in corners, no matter how sexy, wasn't going to cut it.

Except I changed my mind after half a day. I learned a few things about her. She knew the grounds too well. This wasn't her first visit here. She must have been caught the last time because she was clearly terrified of stepping inside. So, after two days, I took the food out of the equation and lured her in.

I'd let her eat and make her comfortable and see what she would do. I had only planned to sit in the corner and watch. But I hadn't calculated an idiot into my plans. Acid burned in my gut at the memory of Peppe's words and deeds. *Spineless fool.* Peppe had always been an irritation. He was a coward. I knew that even before today. But he'd never downright angered me before. Which, in itself, notched up my agitation with the man.

As if my rage latched onto him, the man himself strode over and plopped the food on the table with a thud. The noise was loud in the quiet room. My hand twitched. The imbecile had no care for his own life and was on a mission to get himself killed.

I killed men for the *Cosa Nostra*. I did it without a second thought or a guilty conscience. But killing one of your own was a different thing entirely. It wasn't something I took lightly. If it wasn't necessary, I avoided it. The question remained if I could let him live for putting his grubby hands on her. He was only clearing up my questions with his actions.

I leaned back in my chair, trying to create a physical distance between him and my hand itching for my gun on my right side.

"Dov'è il vino, idiota?" I tried to curb my anger, but it shot out of my body in unprecedented waves.

The girl watched us with her enormous hazel eyes. Her skin was so pale that her eyes shone like marbles from her translucent face. Peppe hesitated for a second. A matter of life and death. He made the right decision. With a huff, he went down to the cellar, his boot-clad thuds echoing in the kitchen.

Fuck. I wasn't in the mood to kill him now. Well, no. That was a lie. I was in the best damn mood to kill him.

Would have done it instantly. I just didn't want to do it in front of her. Even though she had probably seen far worse, for some reason, the dark bruise on her neck was pissing me off. That and she looked like she expected me to shove my dick in her face any moment.

"Come ti chiami?" I growled.

A flicker of recognition sparked in her eyes before she hid it and pressed her pretty pink lips into a thin line.

A shiver of annoyance coiled in my gut. *Did she think I was as much an idiot as the usual men she associated with?* "Cut the crap. I already know you understand us. Don't think I've not seen you listening to the maids talk." The ancient legs of the chair quivered as I rocked in an effort to cool off. "Now, let's try again. Your name..." she opened her mouth, "and don't fucking lie to me." Her mouth snapped shut.

Her face turned red, and her teeth gritted behind her closed lips. Indecision swam in her eyes as she wrestled with her inner thoughts. Then she wrenched the word out, "Florina."

She didn't lie. Even though she wanted to. She didn't. That brought me a spark of joy. If there was one thing I could spot a mile off, it was a lie. I could have said it was a sixth sense I developed in the *Cosa Nostra*. But I already had it long before I met Antonio or his set of men. When you were poor, you were invisible. Yet it gave you the clearest vision of others and their fucking lies.

"Not so difficult, was it?" I mumbled, even though I didn't expect an answer from those tight lips. "Now eat." I nodded towards the food.

Her eyes narrowed, and her mouth squeezed into a

frown. She didn't trust me, but the plate in front was too tempting. I knew the feeling. Pride fighting over hunger. The thing was, hunger always won. Just when I thought she would be the exception, she surprised me and, as per her usual habit, ditched the silver cutlery and started stuffing her mouth.

A stifled groan erupted in my mouth. How can a woman gobbling down pasta with her bare hands be so fucking sexy?

My daydreams of her were interrupted by Peppe coming back up, holding a bottle of wine and a glass.

I glared at him. *Would it be so bad to get rid of the fucker?* His hands froze right above the table.

"Thump it down and there'll be a hole where your mouth was."

His eyes were wild, locked on the gun I was pointing at his mouth. To be fair, I hadn't even realised I was doing it. The girl, Florina, looked up between the two of us and went right on eating. This one had a shitload of guts in her. Peppe swallowed audibly and placed the bottle and glass softly on the table like he was putting a baby to sleep.

"Open it," I ordered, waving the gun in his face.

He pulled out the wine opener from his pocket. The cock popped, and the Bordeaux sloshed all over Antonio's grandfather's dining table as he tried to pour it, staining it red. I hissed and whacked the jerk's head with the metal in my hands.

"Clean the mess up and get the fuck out of here before I slit your body into pieces."

My head was too clouded. *Would Peppe even be*

noticed if he was missing? Explaining it to Antonio would be a bitch, of course.

The woman in front of me was the epitome of calmness while he fumbled like a gawky teenager. She emptied the wine from her glass in one gulp and continued shoving the food like it was a competition. While she chewed and Peppe mopped the table, I focused on the Bordeaux drip edging on the right corner of her lip. The urge to lick it off brought a new level of self-control.

The table was clean, and Peppe's hovering was pissing me off. I wanted her alone. All to myself.

"Fuck off." The fool almost stumbled in his rush to get out of the room. The door banged on his way out as he rushed off to the servants' quarters on the right side of the house.

Finally, it was just me and her. There was a shift in the air like we both became aware of it at the same time. It was heavy and electric. Her hands quivered ever so lightly even though her eyes were bold, watching me while she ate. I couldn't tell if she was scared, anxious, or turned on. Her hair was greasy and dark. I wondered what the colour would be when it got a good wash. Dark brown, I thought. Would it feel soft if I wrapped my fist around it? My cock gave a painful jerk at the thought of it.

She finished her food off in record time. No surprise.

In that time, I had made two decisions.

Florina. I was going to call her Rina. It would sound so much better on my lips when she rode me. Which automatically brought me to the second decision. She was coming with me.

I shoved the chair back and stood up. She immediately jumped up, her body on full alert. I was a big man. Broad and tall. Six feet four, which meant I towered over almost everyone. So, the fact that she was small was no surprise. Something she tried to hide by pulling her chin up and stiffening her stance. It only made her look fragile, like I could break her if a huff of my breath touched her. It didn't stop me from wanting to try.

"Wash your hands." I jerked my head towards the kitchen. "And then you're coming with me."

She didn't argue. She was more resigned, like she knew her fate. I wasn't sure how I felt about that.

I followed her movements as she walked over to the sink. She washed her plate and glass clumsily, like she hadn't handled either in a very long time. Her dress used to be some other colour but was now brown and in tatters. It was three sizes too large on her tiny frame. My imagination ran wild with what she would look like without it.

My tongue darted out, and I licked my lip just as she turned around to wipe her hands on the towel. Her lips stiffened, and her eyes darkened. *Is she scared, or is she turned on?* I wasn't sure which one I wanted it to be. Both, perhaps?

"Let's go." I pulled the kitchen door open and waited for her to walk out. And just because she was *il mio passerotto*, I grasped her arm when she passed me and held her in place. Wouldn't put it past this one to make a run for it, and that would be too bad, wouldn't it?

We left the main villa behind and trudged through the gravel path. Her breath was shallow and uneven.

Mine was calm and deep. The night was dark, and the air cool. Our men lurked around in the shadows, so I kept her to my left between the side parapet wall and my body, hiding her from view.

I knew better. I should have knocked on Rosa's door and handed her over to her. Antonio's trusted maid, with her lifelong service to the family, would have been a good mother figure for Rina. It would have been better for her than coming with me in the dark like my dirty little secret. But I guess even though my suit was clean, my intentions were just that. Dirty.

We were at my little house on the outskirts of the inside boundary in a matter of a few minutes. The front door creaked as I shoved it open, and the dim light painted the tiny hallway with a warm glow. I didn't get attached to many things in my life other than Antonio and his family. But I could say I was oddly attached to my house. It was tiny compared to the villa. But it was mine. The day that Antonio wrote this house under my name was one of the best days of my life. I locked the door behind me and strode further into the living room. Her footsteps followed behind me meekly.

The moment I entered the living room, I heard a soft thud and turned to find her on her knees. *Fuck me!* My brows furrowed even as she reached for my belt. *Cazzo!* I glared down at my hand, fisted in a death grip on hers. "What the fuck you doing?"

I might as well have yelled those words out because everything came to a standstill. My heartbeat, my pulse point. Except for my cock, which throbbed behind the zipper of my pants.

When I found her eyes, they were big and almost luminous as she stared at me with a cooked eyebrow and defiance. "Thanking you."

Disgust crawled all over my skin. I couldn't get away fast enough. Lurching back, I shoved her away from me. Agitation whirled inside me, but years of training made me only show my indifference. "If you want to thank me, use your fucking words," I scoffed. *Liar.* My dick jerked behind my zipper, and my heart pounded in my ribcage like a racehorse galloping to the win.

What the hell was all the jargon falling out of my mouth? Didn't I want her fucking body? *Fuck!* Of course I wanted her.

But not on her fucking knees as a thank you, like she'd thanked all the men before her.

"There's a guest room upstairs with a bathroom," I muttered through my gritted teeth. "Find it and make use of it. I am off to bed."

As I strode upstairs, I didn't know who I was more mad at. Her for offering her services or me for wanting her to want me more than as a mere fucking thank you.

CHAPTER THREE

FLORINA

What just happened? I followed the tight ass stalking up the stairs with my eyes. You'd think I was on fire. He couldn't get away from me fast enough. Now that was something that had never happened before.

Unease rattled my nerves. Too many things happened that were new to me. A man leaving food out for me for days on end. A man putting a gun in another man's face because of me... *I think.* A man refusing my mouth...

I pulled my gaze from his disappearing ass and dropped it to my brown scuffed sneakers. The laces were all twisted, and the plastic on the ends was chipped off. No matter how hard I tried, I couldn't keep the thread together, so it was rapidly piling off, one thread at a time. These sneakers looked as out of place on the blue and white patterned tiled floor as I did standing in his pristine house. Both objects, dirty and damaged, were meant for outside in a dark alleyway. I looked around. Not here.

The house was huge. Not as big as the one I'd had my dinner in, but still, it was large. The shabby house I had lived in for most of my life, which was made from clay and straw, would probably fit into the kitchen and with enough space leftover for another. I did a slow 360-degree turn. Didn't want to move further and stain the pristine floor with the dirt on my feet. It was all so clean and neat and uncluttered. A massive fireplace and a sofa gulped down most of the space in the living room. The sofa was a black leather one. You'd think it would look intimidating. Instead, it looked old and welcoming. Like coming home to a childhood home full of memories. I swallowed the lump in my throat and glanced beyond to peek at the kitchen. Much like the bigger house, a row of dark wooden cabinets and a marble top greeted me. Except the marble here was a dark blue. Blue floors, blue worktops... he'd had a blue tie on... *did the man like blue?*

I sighed. This wasn't me. The man stretched so broad and wide that every time he moved, I thought he would burst out of the suit he wore. It was odd. He moved like he wanted to erupt out of it. Like he didn't like to be entrapped by gentleman's clothes. Like he should be naked... *Stop it.* I didn't wonder about strange men. Because there hadn't been a single man in my life that had been worth wondering about. The last one I wasted my energy on threw harsh words at me like sharp icicles piercing my chest. *You think I'd love a filthy girl like you* echoed off the ivory brick walls of this house, as if those dark words were screamed out just now.

If I craned my neck, I could see the front door at the end of the warmly lit corridor. I knew men. Even before he locked the door and pocketed the key, I thought I knew what he wanted. He and the jackass Albanian would have common ground. Even though I might have been more willing with this one than I was with the Albanian. This one smelled good. Had a faint scruff on him that was polished. The type that you spend time taking care of. Not the type that grew wild because you couldn't afford a razor. But all men wanted one thing and one thing only from me. So I thought I'd get the job done and get out of here. But he hadn't even allowed me to blow him.

This wasn't right. Felt all wrong. It made my skin itch with unease. Made my pulse pump in my ear. I didn't belong here. If a man didn't want the one thing I had to give, then he didn't want me at all. Not a shred of hesitance veiled my thoughts before I marched over to the kitchen and grabbed the biggest knife from the knife block. I would have normally taken the smallest one. It was faster to defend myself. But he was massive, and I'd need a bigger knife to do the job.

I didn't know his name or what he did or how he was related to the Capizzi brothers. But he must have been because he was hot. Short, almost cropped black hair cut close to his head in tiny spirals. Thick black eyebrows with the most beautiful brown eyes I'd ever seen matched with a long, sharp nose and the scruff on his jaw that had a pulse ticking somewhere in my body where it had lain long forgotten.

What was happening? I shook myself visibly. I did

not pay attention to men. Definitely not their fucking faces. If I did, it was their body, so I could judge how I could defend myself. He was tall. Like really tall. Six feet and a few inches tall. As if that wasn't bad enough, he was broad. The muscles that had bulged underneath his suit told me he knew how to use his body to suck the last breath of life from someone. Someone like me. That should be my worry now. Not how he wore his suit like armour. Not how the ink seeping out from under his white cuff contrasted against his olive skin. Definitely not his long, thick fingers. Because that made me wonder about other long, thick things on him.

"Fuck!" I kicked the cabinet door in front of me. This wasn't helping.

"It's all a charade," I muttered. Just like he clothed himself in a starched shirt and hid a graveyard of black tattoos underneath, he was hiding something, and he was going to be more dangerous than the men with open lust in their eyes.

With the knife clutched in my right hand, I checked out other non-existent exits in the house. All locked, of course. So I sneaked up the creaking stairs that gave me away louder than a drum roll. Good thing I had the knife because if he hadn't heard me kick his furniture earlier, he definitely heard me coming upstairs. I counted four doors. The one furthest down the hall was the only one with a closed door. The first open door to my left showed an office of some kind. Even the table was clean. Not a shred of paper out of place. The next one was a bedroom, and across from it was a toilet. So I guessed Prince Charming was sleeping behind the fourth door. The only one closed. But he wasn't Prince Charming, was he? He wasn't blond, and he wasn't charming. He was rude, and he was hot as fuck. I wouldn't have minded sucking him off. Finally, a dick I actually wanted in my mouth. Except he didn't want me to.

With a huff, I marched to the bedroom, not his one, of course, and slammed the door shut. The old door shivered on its hinges before creaking into place. What was his plan, anyway? I flipped the lock on the door and looked around. A bed, a three-door dark wooden cupboard with an oval mirror in the middle door, and a small desk and a chair in the corner.

He might have been hot as fuck, but men only wanted one thing. Dropping the knife on the bed, I shoved the desk towards the door, my teeth on edge as an uneven metal nail underneath scraped along the floor. *Cristo.* My eyes followed the fresh grove zigzagging on the wooden floor. The man had been so kind, and I had gone and broken his... hold on. *Had he been kind?* Unease crawled all over me. I didn't do kindness. People weren't kind unless they wanted something from me. So he wanted something from me, or he wasn't kind. I carried the chair and stacked it on top of the desk. That would teach him if he was planning to come for a nightly visit.

Satisfied, I moved to the adjoining door and flipped it open. *Well, fuck me!* The room had an adjoining bathroom and the fucking office attached to it. How was I going to barricade this?

Frustration itched on my skin. The bathroom was tempting, but there was no way I could let my guard down to take a shower. Couldn't he have just let me blow him and sent me on my way? No! He had to defy the norm of the spectrum of men I knew.

Think, Florina, he must want something.

I paced the floor. Bedroom, bathroom, and office. Pause. Office, bathroom, and bedroom.

He didn't want me to jerk him off.

He was definitely not being kind because, let's face it, no one ever was.

So what...

I stopped. In the middle of the bathroom. Realisation dawned, and the navy blue tiles on the walls laughed at my stupidity. He thought he was too good for me. He wanted to be a good Samaritan, but I wasn't good enough for him.

Anger pooled inside me, and a rush of heat throttled through my skin. I fucking hated men who thought they were too good for me. I had many talents. I was a brilliant thief. Snagging a man's wallet point blank with his eyes on me was a practised art. I was an excellent liar. I had proved it innumerable times. But above all, I was a master at sucking men's dicks. The fact that this man didn't want me to was frankly offensive. If he thought anyone could do a better job than me... I didn't even realise I'd marched through the office and hallway until I yanked his door open and barrelled into his room without even thinking of bringing the big fucking knife I was going to use to defend my honor. *Really, Florina... where's your head?*

Midnight blue walls, an orange, glowing tabletop lamp, and a massive bed in the middle were what I should have focused on. Instead, my gaze zoomed in on the man on the bed with a naked tattooed torso and a clear hard-on under the crisp sapphire sheets.

"What the fuck are you doing?"

Căcat. He was huge. I knew that much, even without lifting the sheets. And wide. Ink ran up the entire length of both his arms, and on his left breast, a tattooed skull resided, begging for my starved mouth. Intricate words circled around it, too far for me to read, hanging onto a circle of drawings like the fine artwork of a Mayan temple somewhere.

"Rina."

"Urgh." I scowled at him darkly. He leaned on his elbows, looking at me with slitted and glittering angry eyes. "Who the fuck is Rina?"

I guessed I wasn't worthy of an answer because all he did was glare at me. What the fuck was he angry about? I crossed my arms and glared right back at him. I didn't know how long we stood at a standoff, but it felt like it took a hundred pulse beats before he dropped his head to the pillow with a heavy sigh and growled a "get out" to me.

Not that easy, buddy.

"You know... that looks painful to me..." I jerked my head towards the very obvious bulk under the sheet. "If you didn't want to act like such a goody-two-shoes, I could take care of that for you." I don't know why the thought of it made my lips dry. I also totally didn't lick my lips to tempt him. But it worked like magic.

His expression shifted. It glowered at me in the darkness, and then he rasped two words that told me I had him right where I wanted him. "Come here."

I shrugged that small disappointment coasting somewhere in my veins and strolled over to the bed. He had an arm folded behind his head, and he used his other to curl his fingers towards him.

Here, I had thought he was an exception to mankind. At least this I knew how to do. I knew what to expect, and there weren't any surprises later on. Kindness, my ass. I dropped onto the bed and crawled over to his side.

My God. The man smelled good. I was so used to my stench from days of not washing that it took some time for a pleasant smell to reach my nostrils. But when it did, it was all I could do not to drop down and snuggle up to him. He reminded me of burned charcoal. Dark and musty. And expensive. My gaze locked into his. His burned hot. My hands clutched the sheet right next to his hip. My knuckles grazed his hot skin. I tugged. Nothing. Confused, I glanced down to find his hands clamped onto mine. *What the hell?* Before I could put words into my mouth, he'd yanked me close to him, arm, sheet, and all. I wobbled precariously on top of his chest, trying not to fall on him.

"I'm not the men you know, *Il mio passerotto.* I want to sink my cock into you and make you scream with pleasure." *What?* I jerked back. "So you want to fuck me? Then the game is on. But you want to thank me—" he shoved me off him, and I landed on my ass. "Then do us both a favour and get the hell out of my room."

CHAPTER FOUR

FLORINA

Soft light flickered in, finding cracks through the navy blue curtains. The window was half the size of the wall. But the curtains touching in the middle were enough to give me a peek. Finally. It was daytime.

Above me was a pure white ceiling with cracked plaster and a rosette in the middle, holding a rusty, dull gold lamp. On top were twelve small lights holding fake candles. All twelve of them were lit because I'd left it like that. Beneath me was a mattress so soft it might as well have been a cloud passing by. *Was this a nightmare or what?*

I sat up straight like a whip had cracked my back. This wasn't my life. I was on borrowed time.

I wasn't born for comfort. I had got to twenty-five years without a brush of comfort tainting my skin. I was made for harsh winters and freezing nights. Comfort would make me soft. Weak. Would make me rely on something I could never have.

With a huff, I pushed off the soft cotton sheet on top of me and sat on the side of the bed. I might have slept for two hours tops. Drifting in and out because I didn't trust the man. I refused to trust the man.

The desk and the chair still stood guard where I'd parked them. But there were noises creeping underneath my door, which reminded me yet again that I was in a house with a man who apparently wanted to fuck me.

I want to sink my cock into you and make you scream with pleasure.

His words taunted me as I padded to the bathroom. I peed and crossed to the sink to wash my face, where I found a toothbrush and a tube of toothpaste. Palpitations picked up in my heart, and a frown wrinkled my forehead. This wasn't there last night. A towel hung next to the shower, and there were pretty bottles in the shower. Men's stuff. Not that I was choosy. So he'd come in here and put this shit in here, and I hadn't heard him. Did he come inside the room? Unease is a nasty bitch. It messes you up and makes you do rash things.

I need to get the hell out of here.

I stormed through his office, ran down the stairs, and stopped short in the kitchen. *Bloody hell.* With his bare back to me, he walked around in the kitchen. *Cooking?* The man was wearing jeans so low they were in danger of falling from his olive-skinned hips. My eyes stubbornly refused to move from where the dark blue of his jeans met his skin. He couldn't be wearing boxers underneath. Could he? A tug was all that would take to...

"*Buongiorno, il mio passerotto.*"

Silver buttons on his jeans and the thickness behind them met me as he turned around. My eyes jerked up so fast I was in danger of swaying to the floor like a fucking damsel in distress.

"I'm not your fucking sparrow," I snapped, partly to cover my embarrassment but also because I wasn't a fucking bird. Birds were weak. I was not.

His eyes met mine with a wicked smile in them. I refused to shift and kept them pasted to his. No matter how tempting it was to drop down to his delicious bare torso. I didn't need to see it. Last night's memory was all too fresh. He would have heard me plonking down the stairs a mile off. The least he could have done was put on a damn shirt if he had good intentions. Which just proved the point that he didn't. But then again, he had made his intentions pretty clear to me. *I want to sink my cock into you and make you scream with pleasure.* There was no misunderstanding that.

"Time to eat up." He piled two plates with eggs and bacon from the pan he was holding in his massive hand.

Massive hand, massive... No, I wasn't going to go down that line. My mouth watered. For the food, that is, but I refused to indulge.

The plate scraped against the marble top as he shoved it towards me. "I'm sure it'll put you in a good mood."

"I'm in a good mood."

He wiped his hand slowly over his lips. "I can see that." *Was he laughing at me?* Last night, he'd been harsh. Now he was in a good mood at the expense of mine. I wasn't a fucking joke. I opened my mouth to tell him just that... "Eat up. Now." His voice flipped to cold and clipped. I was sure he had an army who'd listen to that voice, but not me. I reared up to tell him that, and he sighed like he'd seen into the future. "Please. You can have your fight after."

My lips thinned. Fine. I would eat and then I was getting out of here. Disregarding his precious silverware, I dug into the bacon with my bare hands. My dirty hands and chipped nails tingled, and I just knew that his gaze was on them. I waited. When nothing came out, I looked up with a scowl.

"What?"

He pulled his gaze away from my hands and picked up his fork and knife. "Well, what?"

"Aren't you going to order me to use your metal pieces?" I noticed the yellow of the egg dripping and took the side of my right hand and licked it from the bottom to the top.

My sole purpose had been to taunt him. But it felt weirdly like that backfired on me. He shifted behind the island he was leaning on, and his eyes darkened to black slits. His voice was thick and rough when he lied. "You have beautiful hands. You can use them however you want."

"Liar," I mumbled.

"Shut up and eat," he ordered.

Even though he didn't correct me, the soft pulp behind the metal armour of my heart throbbed like a trapped bird. *Fuck!* I wasn't going to be his little bird.

Everything in the room was loud. The clatter of his cutlery on a porcelain plate. The bite of crusty bacon in my mouth. The gulp of hot coffee going down my throat. The agitation in my breaths that came out in a huff.

Căcat! I *was* a bird, and I was trapped.

Each mouthful that I took felt like a year off my life. Unease prodded my skin like a thousand rose thorns scraping across it. Nine gulps later, I was done and shoved the plate towards him. He caught it on instinct rather than sight right before it hit the floor, sliding the last bit of bacon into his mouth with his other hand. There wasn't a flicker of anger on his face as he piled the plates and dumped them into the sink.

"Let me out," I spoke to his back.

He did the dishes as if he was hard of hearing.

"Let me out!" My tone rang loud, like a fire drill in a tiny hall.

His movements were calm as he dried his hands and turned around. With his forearms on the counter, he rested, leaning back, looking for all the world completely relaxed. The waistline of his jeans dipped down another inch, showing off the visible V on either side of his hips. "Stay."

I jerked back in my seat. He could have shot me, and I would have been less surprised. "I'm not a fuck toy."

"I know that."

What was wrong with this man? "Here's the deal." I leaned forward. "I'll blow you, and then you let me go."

His posture remained the same, but his stare was dark and intent. There was a tick on his jaw and a tension in his arms that told me I'd angered him. Again. But his words were quiet even though they felt loud in my ears. "No."

"Well, why the hell not? I'm not going to fuck you."

"Yes. You are."

Jackass! He was full of himself. "What are you going to do? Ra—"

He was up straight and leaning towards my face in a few strides. "Don't even think of saying it. I will never do anything against your will."

He was too much. His words. His deeds. My hands fisted on the countertop, and I leaned away from him. I needed a break. And I needed a wash.

His hand fell down like a ton of bricks and wrapped around mine. "Stay." I startled, looking at our joined hands. His clean-cut nails and fingers with a dark dusting of hair and three metal rings. My stained hands lined with filth and mud-lined fingernails. Littered with scratches but still fragile and bony.

Sudden emotion filled me like a gush of water filling an empty tank. "Why?"

"Because I want you to. There's food in the fridge. A comfortable bed. Take a shower. Enjoy yourself."

He looked at me like my past didn't exist. Like I was born wrapped in a gold cloth and not in a cold cot. He looked at me like I was a precious stone and not the shit under his Armani shoes. I thought that he needed a doctor. Someone to check his eyes and clear his vision. Because his vision wasn't right. It was showing him a mirage and the reality he wouldn't like. But his look didn't change, and it only riddled me with more unease. I jerked my hand off him and crossed my arms in front of me. "You think I stink?"

He let out a harsh laugh and shook his head. "Then don't take a shower. It was just a suggestion."

I scowled at him. The man was not only an idiot, but he should get his senses tested. Because even I knew I needed a shower. A shower did sound good, though. "I'll think about it," I told him haughtily.

If he forced me, I was out of here. But he didn't. He stepped away from me, and I didn't know why, but I suddenly felt the cavity in between us.

"Do me a favour—" *and here come the requirements.* I scowled at him. "Stay inside. I can't protect you if you are caught around the villa. Please?"

CHAPTER FIVE

FLORINA

The window outside was stained with droplets, and my insides churned with emotions. The echo of the soft thud of a closing door and a key turning in the lock crawled into my body and vibrated throughout. The man was no idiot. He knew if I really wanted to, I'd find a way to sneak out of his house. The lock on the window in the laundry room was the first one I would try. The question was, really, if I wanted to.

"I can't protect you if you are caught around the villa. Please?"

The words 'protect' and 'please' whirled in my heart, making me feel giddy. No one had ever requested something from me, let alone wanted to protect me.

It was wrong. What he wanted from me was wrong. But would it hurt to pretend for one day? Pretend that this house was mine. Me, the happy woman painting her nails while her man was at work? I looked at my nails and decided it would. Pretend play never brought anything but heartache, and my nails were so chipped the polish would peel off before it touched the surface. Every instinct of mine told me to get out of here. Forget the man. *For fuck's sake.* I didn't even know his name. And I was planning to play house with him. So I ignored all of that and stayed.

Because I never listened, and taking risks was second nature to me. When Tata was drunk and wasted, I would still goad him because that was who I was. When Mama brought her clients home, I didn't shy away but yelled my displeasure at her. I didn't care about getting hurt. So I wasn't going to now either.

Besides, the man may have been delusional and not think I smelled. But a sniff in the wrong direction might have killed me from my own stink before he ever got the chance to.

So I did something I had never done before. I did something for myself. I went upstairs with the full intention of taking a shower. But I accidentally bumped into his bath... fine. I sneaked into his room to check it out and found a bath in his bathroom. So, I did another one of those 'first' things.

I soaked in it for hours. Then I emptied it completely, refilled it, and filled it with his smells. By the end of it, I wanted to smell like burned charcoal, too. My skin wrinkled from the water. It burned where I took a hard brush and scrubbed all over. It might have also been because I had found the brush in his storeroom, and it was meant to brush sidewalks with, not skin. But it didn't matter.

For once in my life, I wanted to be clean. I paused while I pushed the rough hair of the brush in between my toes to find the hidden dirt. *Did I want to make myself pretty for him?* The thought crossed my mind that I wanted to be anything that he would want. *Whatever.* I shouldn't care. I was doing what I wanted to.

By the time I pulled myself out of the bath, my skin burned red, and my hair was dry and empty of any greasiness. The only disappointment was I still didn't smell like burned charcoal. I smelled more like... I sniffed my skin. Normal. Pretty. Like lemon and pine.

I came out of the bathroom exhausted. I needed a nap. The fact that I hadn't slept much last night might have also been the underlying cause. But I didn't look into too many details. I wasn't one of those doctors who could look inside a human brain.

I just did nice things for myself. What had he said? Enjoy yourself. So I did by plonking down on his bed and taking a nap for a few hours. Mine was all dirty and smelly because some filthy girl had slept in it last night. But his smelled fresh and like him, all male and feral. It was much better here.

When I woke up, the sun was gliding down, and my stomach was rumbling. For once, I had had ample food within reach but hadn't bothered to eat. What an idiot.

It was quiet in the kitchen. Emotion prickled in my throat. I couldn't remember the last time I had cooked. Well, I did. I cooked the last day Mama was alive. Tata was already dead by then. Alcohol really did ruin a man's life. But I was stuck with my mother. I cooked. She keeled over and died. I buried her, then I guess I got lost and didn't make it back to the wretched neighbourhood with the vile memories. Even when I was so hungry I could have bitten off my hand to eat it, I never regretted that decision.

But this kitchen reminded me of how much I loved to cook. How long it had been since I had made something nice. Suddenly, I wanted to make something nice. For him. *If he didn't want me to suck him off, then I'd at least cook him something so good he'd want to keep me.* I smacked my head with my hand. I had no idea why I thought that.

MARCO

Antonio's stare was sharp and pinned to me from his chair behind his desk. My poker face hid the guilt coasting inside my body. I'd never hidden anything from the man. But for some reason that I didn't even know, I kept my new little secret to myself.

I was wrong. She wasn't a bird. She was a fucking coconut. One I was going to have a hard time breaking open to get to her soft insides. But it wasn't going to stop me from trying.

I wiped the amusement off my lips and shuffled uncomfortably in the chair across from his desk. I had a feeling he got these chairs down from his house in Boston for one purpose alone, and that was to make me uncomfortable. How was my broad body going to fit in this ridiculous thing with arms? Design, they called it.

"What's up with you?"

Lots of things. Like a fucking coconut that needed to be cracked open. But I only gave him the reason I wanted to.

"There's an Albanian looming around the property. I need to get rid of him."

His stare instantly warped from sharp to murderous. My boss was a patient man. Except when it came to the safety of his wife and children. He leaned forward with a dangerous glint in his eyes. "How the fuck did he get so close?"

"A hole in the metal fencing." One no doubt made by *la mia piccola cocco*. Which reminded me she now had two weapons to assault me with. Pliers she'd probably had with her to cut the fence and the big knife I'd noticed missing in my kitchen. Ah, *la mia piccola cocco*. She warmed my heart like no one ever had. What didn't was the security footage I'd looked at to see the Albanian following Rina into the property. I didn't need to know the details to know it was another man who wanted to get his dick sucked by my woman. The line was getting fucking long.

There was a knock on the door, and Peppe came in with Antonio's espresso. The man drank at least one per hour. One every ten minutes if he was in a bad mood. It was just my luck that today seemed to be one of those days. I didn't need his death stares on me. Not today.

I concentrated on not killing Peppe instead as he made his way with the espresso vibrating in his hand. The air in the room hummed with his uneasiness. It took him three fucking steps. That's all before the espresso ended up painting the fucking floor.

"What the fuck's wrong with you?" Antonio grunted as Peppe dropped to his knee, shaking from head to toe. I hid the wicked grin behind my hand as I watched him trying to clean up the mess. How could this idiot make this mess... well, messier? "Fuck this. Get me another one." Peppe took to Antonio's words like a siren blasting his freedom and hurled outside the room.

The chuckle I'd been holding in broke free.

"What's so funny? What's got into everyone? You're acting fucked up, and Peppe looks like he'd had a gun to his face."

My chuckle died down fast. *Cazzo.* The man was very close to the truth. "The real question is, why are you in a foul mood?" I asked to distract him. "I thought Aria slept through the night."

"She did," he told me with a proud smile, which instantly changed into a wicked grin. "So I had an all-nighter with Divya."

I shook my head. "Of course you did. Like you'd even think of actually getting some sleep."

"I did. But have you seen my wife?"

I knew better than to answer that. Antonio's jealousy knew no bounds. Plus, I was fucking tired of hearing about all the action everyone was getting except me.

La mia piccola cocco. I wondered what she was up to. I really hoped she hadn't sneaked off. I shuffled out of the chair. "I'm off."

He stood up and gathered his files together. "Bring the Albanian in."

"No."

His hands halted, and his sharp gaze pulled to mine. A million excuses ran through my mind. He followed her. He could have killed her. He could have fucked her. *Fuck*. Maybe he fucked her already. Raped her. But I couldn't tell him any of that.

I guess it was my lucky day. Because the man who brought me in and gave me a life to live for decided yet again to trust me fully. Even though I was unworthy of it right now.

"Fine. Get rid of him then."

I nodded and stalked over to the door.

"Marco." His stern voice hit my back, and my hands involuntarily clenched around the handle.

"Sì." I didn't turn around. Didn't trust my poker face right now.

"You'll have your reasons, I am sure. When you're ready, you'll tell me."

It wasn't an order, even if he wanted it to sound like one. It was a reassurance that no matter what, he still had my back.

With a nod, I strode out the door.

My boot-clad right foot rested on my left knee. The green iron bench was cold on my ass, but I couldn't say I felt it. I was all hot and burning with silent rage. The Albanian I'd tied to the tree was getting on my fucking nerves.

One, the fucker had a thick layer of meat on him. I'd

busted my knuckles in several places, taking him down. Two, the filth coming out of his mouth was riling me up. The uncontrollable rage I had lived with until Antonio calmed me down was throbbing in my veins. Only a thin layer of control kept it veiled from the world. Someone should have warned the fucker about this.

"She's a fucking liar! A thief. She stole my—"

"Careful," I admonished quietly, my gaze on the speck of filth under my nails and intent on taking it out with my sharp-edged knife. Couldn't stand filth. Reminded me of all the filth I had come across in my previous life. Made me wonder why the mud coating *la mia cocco* didn't bother me, then.

"Watch. Fucking bitch."

My gaze shot to him. He was going to get himself killed. Sooner rather than later. I wanted it to be later. Much, much later.

"She thinks she's too fucking good. She wanted to suck me off but didn't want to fuck."

My hand fisted around my knife. *Deep breaths, Marco. Slower means more pain.*

His bloodied eye watched me intently. "Why would a nice man like you want to get involved with her? She's a fucking whore."

Fucker. I swirled my arm and flipped the knife. Why couldn't he have given me the pleasure of killing him slowly?

With a sigh, I got up and strolled over to him. The seeping bloody hole in his throat and my knife in the middle of it looked like an artwork but didn't bring me any pleasure. Nor the bulged-out eyes of a dead man. I should have cut him to pieces and put him on a barbecue. Now that would have been a better way of killing him. Instead, I was resigned to pulling my knife out as red sprayed my clean white shirt and black suit.

"See. Not such a nice man, after all," I told the dead man as I wiped my knife clean on his sweat-soaked shirt. Holding the knife up as a mirror, I cleaned my face. Couldn't have my woman seeing my fucked-up face.

I found my men where I'd left them fifty meters away. "Get rid of the body."

A pang of anticipation filled me as I made my way to my house. This was the first time that I was looking forward to going home. The question was if she was going to be home or prove she was, in fact, a bird and that she'd flown away.

CHAPTER SIX

MARCO

The door swung against the wall as I stepped into my tiny foyer. A smell in the air told me something was cooking. My heart thumped in anticipation, but my feet were lazy as I strolled into the kitchen and found *la mia piccola cocco* in it.

Fuck! My heart zapped like the metal paddles of a defibrillator had touched my chest. *She was here.* In my home. In the fucking kitchen. Cooking. Wearing one of my shirts. The shirt touched her knees. I'd never wished I'd been shorter until now. If I'd been shorter, I would have got a more interesting show. *What the fuck am I thinking?*

She must have sensed I was there but ignored me entirely. She went around with her cooking like I was a fucking ghost. I didn't care. *She was here.* I watched as she set the pan on the table. Some kind of stew steamed in it. She dumped two plates on the table. Her movements were jerky and rough. She opened the drawer, gathered up a bunch of cutlery, and dumped it on top of what I assumed must have been my plate. The chair scraped out on her side, and she plopped down. Three heartbeats passed before she pulled her gaze finally to me. Whatever she was going to say froze in her mouth as her gaze thinned on my shirt. I followed her gaze and realised I'd forgotten to clean up. My white shirt looked like Pollock had a go at it. Any woman I knew would have fainted at the sight. Not this one, though.

"Are you coming or not?" Her tone was snappy, but her gesture was loving.

I wanted to get on my knees and thank her for not fucking leaving. Instead, I took my seat and shifted through the cutlery under her sharp gaze. The first mouthful of food glided down my throat like a warm flush of a memory. The stew was fucking delicious. But I may have been biased in my opinion. *"È delizioso."*

She blinked like it was the first time she'd ever received a compliment. The fact that it probably was sparked a flame in my black heart.

I'd taken five mouthfuls before I realized she hadn't started. She was too busy fumbling with her fork and knife, subtly trying to mirror me.

"You want to learn how to use them?"

Her teeth were clenched as she muttered, "I have to."

"That's not what I asked."

Her gaze was down, eyeing the cutlery like it was venom in her hands, kept in control by her tightly fisted, small hands. Her chin wobbled as she whispered, "Yes."

I was out of the chair and leaning behind her in a

matter of a second. She finally asked for help. I knew from my past life what a big step it was to do that. My gigantic hands dropped onto her small ones. Tanned and scratched skin against pale and soft ones. "Relax," I crooned right next to her ear as I soothed her hands and adjusted them around the fork and knife. The tiny hair below her hairline tickled my scruff. Her smell wafted temptingly around my nostrils. Fuck. She smelled good. Like pine and lemon mixed with the memories of a bonfire. I didn't think I had any shower products like that, but I was now going to link this smell to her.

I pushed her index finger on the knife. "Bit more strength here to cut." I let go of her hands and rested mine on the table, enclosing her. "Now try it out."

She fumbled for a minute, and then she got it. My heart thumped with pride. Hers was heavy as she breathed. With a sigh, I moved away and finished off my meal.

It wasn't a fancy restaurant. There was no music. I was in my blood-spattered clothes, and she was wearing my shirt. Yet I couldn't say I had ever enjoyed any meal more.

I finished first. She dropped her cutlery with a clatter, swiped her finger with the last bit of gravy, and licked it off. An uncontrolled growl escaped me. She halted mid-lick as if she hadn't realised what she was doing. Her gaze told me she was waiting for me to reprimand her. If only she knew how much my cock jerked watching her.

When I didn't say anything, she did it three fucking times, and it was like every lick was a tug on my cock.

Finally, she was done. Her plate was clean, my boxers were wet.

"I can suck you off," she said in a sultry tone that was maddening, and my control shook like a building trembling on its foundation. Until her next words hit me like a fist to my face. "To thank you."

Of course, she had to fucking say those words.

A scrape and a crash, and my chair was on the floor. I stumbled back a few feet like she'd physically attacked me. "You don't have to suck anyone off for fucking food, Rina." Frustration crawled in my body, hot and itchy, ready to spill out.

My steps were harsh and heavy as I made my way angrily to my room and slammed the door shut. The wood vibrated angrily on the rusty hinges, warning me that the house was old and needed tender love. I ignored it and slammed the bathroom door twice as hard as I shed my clothes and jumped into a scalding hot shower. I wasn't sure what bore my wrath the most. Me for wanting her. Her for not wanting me. Or the fucking situation we were in. I didn't want to be yet another man she dropped on her knees for as a fucking thank you. I wanted to be the only man she spread her legs for because she wanted me like I wanted her.

The harsh water hit me like pins, and my cock throbbed between my legs to tell me it didn't care for my morals. A groan grated through my throat as I pictured her on her knees with my cock between those pretty pink lips. *No.* I jerked my hand off it and washed myself off. Off of any thoughts of her and off of the dirt and blood on my skin.

I needed to be patient with her. It had only been a day. She needed more time.

I dried myself off roughly and dumped the towel carelessly on the floor. My eyes thinned on the bath. There was a dried line of water that told me someone had taken a bath recently. My razor lay discarded in the middle of it, and my toothbrush was next to it. Of course, she didn't use any of the stuff I had left for her. I wanted to be annoyed, but a warmth entered the cavities of my heart.

My breath paused for a second in my bedroom. Why the fuck did this room smell of her? Then I noticed the rumpled sheets that had been made up this morning, and I just knew she had slept in here. My hard-on was back.

"Fuck," I cursed loudly to no one and plonked on the bed. How was I going to get any sleep now? I concentrated on breathing without inhaling. *I would not smell her. I would not smell her. Fuck.* My breath released, and she was all over my bed.

I needed to get out of here. Get out of here before I crawled to her and gave in to her enticing offer. I was lifting myself off the bed on my elbows when the door swung quietly open to reveal the woman of the hour.

"What the fuck do you want now?" My tone was harsh, but my patience had run out.

Her hand on the doorknob stayed, but her body pulled visibly away.

I sighed and ran a frustrated hand through my still wet hair. She just needed more time. "I'm sorry. I didn't mean to sound harsh." I softened my tone. "What do you want?'

Her gaze was on my dick. There wasn't a sheet this time, and nothing blocked her view of my stiff cock. I sighed. *Thanks, fellow.*

"I want to—"

"No."

Her shoulders stiffened, and she took a step into the room. *No. No.* "What if I want to?"

"Want to what?" I growled.

"Fuck you."

Well, fuck me! I wanted to jump off the bed and crawl all over her. Instead, I fisted my hands on the sheet and thinned my gaze at her. "Swear to God, woman, there's no going back from this. No running away and definitely no sucking another man's dick. *Sì?*"

Her hands clenched on the bottom of my shirt and crushed it into a million pieces. I sighed. Who was I kidding? This wasn't going to happen. She wasn't going to allow the guard she'd put up around her to come crashing down because I fucking wanted her. "Go to your room, *la mia piccola cocco*," I said softly as I dropped back to my bed.

"Why?"

Jesus. Could she not take a hint? I covered my face with my hand. Breathing in. Praying for patience and, for once in my life, to do the right thing. "Why what?"

"Why do you want me?" Her voice rang thin and uncertain in the room, and the air cleared around me, showing her fears and discomfort. My eyes were closed, but it felt like I was looking into her soul.

My hand slipped off my face, and my gaze met hers. Tension thumped in between us like the drums of a tribe.

Want ached inside my soul, desire burned so hot that it was palpable and pulled like a cord between us. Underneath all that was a need that pulsed. One I couldn't really put my finger on.

A gentleman would quote poetic words and lure her in with promises. I wasn't a gentleman, and I wasn't a liar. My voice was hoarse when I spoke, like I'd spoken a million words before. But they were stretched to the limit, hoping they showed her my soul. "Fuck if I know. Maybe because you remind me of myself. Is that good enough?"

She nodded, her head bobbing up and down slowly, her brown eyes big pools on her face. The room was quiet, and the energy drained out of me like the blood water out the drain a few minutes ago.

"Now go, *la mia piccola cocco.*" I swung my forearm on top of my eyes. Couldn't make the effort to watch her go.

The door swung shut, but the sound of her bare feet padding towards the bed rippled through to my heart.

"You sure about this?" I mumbled through my closed eyes. I couldn't say I didn't try.

"Yes."

Hell yes. I lunged towards her.

CHAPTER SEVEN

FLORINA

C*ăcat!*

The 'yes' I uttered burned the front of me like a blast of hot desert air.

His gaze was so intent it made my heart do a slow dance. One heartbeat was all I had to catch the look in his eyes. It sparked and thundered like a dark storm. The next heartbeat, he lunged for me, and I landed on his bed, flat on my back. Only this time, he was on top. Big, naked, and hard.

I bit my lower lip to put a stop to this intense feeling rushing through me. Stop the rush of pleasure with pain. His eyes shimmered, and before a breath could be released, his lips landed on mine.

A long time ago, I shared my first kiss with my first and only boyfriend. It lasted a day before he threw me out, but he was Italian. Tobia. His was the only kiss I had ever enjoyed. My memories exaggerated the pleasure, and

I never thought I would find anything that could equal it. It paled drastically, like faded ink on ancient paper, because this man... *Fuck. I think this was his job. Kissing was his job.* Because he excelled at it like he'd studied it at some fancy college. He wasn't gentle or soft. He was harsh and hard. Intense. He pulled my lips into his, and he bit like I was his favorite dessert and he was too greedy to wait. Then he came in for the kill and slid his tongue inside and, fuck me. How was I ever going to go back to normal again? He took my breath, blasted it with heat, and stuffed it back so that my insides burned like molten lava. Agitation, hot and needy, sparked through my veins and pulsed like an insistent ringing in between my legs. *What the fuck was he doing?* My hands were wrapped around his body, and there was a needy cry like a cat in heat bouncing off the walls. *Cristo.* I think it was coming from me.

I didn't even know this man's name, and I was... *Wait!*

I put my hands in between us, pushed him off, and managed to create a distance of a few breaths. His breathing was harsh and rough and mingled with my own painful gasps.

"What?" His tone grated on my skin like sandpaper.

"Your name?"

He frowned at me like I'd gone insane. He was right. I sucked off men who I didn't want to know. But I wasn't going to be my mama and fuck a man whose name I didn't know. "I don't know your name."

"Cazzo," he groaned, pushing up to his knees in between my legs. His hands gripped my naked thighs, his

shirt bunched between his fists. He dragged his eyes to mine and dissolved me into a quivering mess under his warm stare. "Marco Bova," he said softly as if his dick wasn't an inch away from my pussy. As if we'd just met at a fancy party.

"Marco." I tried it out, and it sounded strange and thick on my tongue. I liked the sound of it. It sounded hot and thick like he was. More than that, I think he liked the sound of his name on my mouth because his gaze shifted to feral.

He fumbled with the buttons on his shirt. All it took was one button to pop, and my pussy greeted him. Naked. Because obviously, I wasn't going back to my dirty underwear. But it must have been a surprise for him. His gaze burned at the edges, a harsh intake of a breath, and he ripped open his own shirt like an overexcited kid with a Christmas toy. The tearing of fabric ripping was louder than the panting of our breaths. But it wasn't enough to hide my embarrassment of lying naked beneath him. My pussy ached to be filled. Still, as the girl who'd been let down too many times, I waited for the other shoe to drop. The insults to fly.

"Sei stupenda, mio piccolo cocco," his voice rasped. His breath gasped. His gaze burned on my skin, heated my tits, and made my nipples shoot straight up.

I wasn't gorgeous, and I was definitely not his fucking coconut, but for one night, I was going to pretend I was.

MARCO

Cazzo. They say God created some women with one man in mind. I wasn't a believer, but that changed one second ago. The man above had me in mind when he created this fucking beauty lying beneath me. Her skin was pale and shone like moonlight on my bed. Her tits were huge and nestled so perfectly in my cupped hands. My rough hands trailed her flat belly, her bony hip, and palmed over her pussy. It glistened like a pink pearl, all freshly shaven. The thought that she used my razor to shave her fucking pussy had my dick jerking with pre-cum.

I was wild and all over her. This was my last meal, and I devoured her just like the man above would have wanted. I sucked and nibbled on her breasts. If I died here from suffocation, I would have died a happy man. And the best part? She was the one stuffing my face with her tits. Not a 'lie down and give it to me' type, my girl. She wiggled under me, rocked her pussy against my dick, and was seemingly intent on leaving a whole track on my back with the sharp edge of her nails. I didn't care. She could mark me anywhere she wanted. Her skin was so soft it felt like silk against my rough sandpaper hands. The callouses in my fingers left trails on her body. She didn't seem to mind, and I was too far gone to care. Slow wasn't a word I knew. Soft, not a thought on my mind. I bit her tit and stuck a finger inside her. My eyes closed in pure joy. *La mia cocco.* She was just as I imagined her to be. All soft inside.

"More," she moaned into my neck, and I obliged. Two fingers, and then three. I pumped into her, wildly bestowing nibbles in between her tits while she pulled my hair as if her life depended on it. *At this rate, I might not have any hair left by tomorrow.* Didn't care either way. She pulsed on my fingers and throbbed around my hand. Then she peaked, and she came, and my God. If this wasn't heaven, I didn't know what was.

I didn't allow her to come down. Couldn't. Somehow, I managed to grab a rubber, and she was as frantic as I was in getting it on me. Her hands fumbled on my dick, and I roughly pushed her off. I thought I might combust, and that was only a possibility inside of her. I moved on top of her and thrust inside, and both our gasps filled the room like a loud echo in an empty cave. Loud, long, and deep.

Fuck! I was never allowing her out of here. She was mine. Mine to fuck and mine to keep. I pulled her ass in and pushed her flat with one hand on her tits. Sweat beaded my forehead as I pumped. I wished I could say it was a long ride. But we were too wild. She squeezed my cock and came like a greedy woman, and I followed right behind her, throttling and choking as my dick jerked inside her. That was single-handedly the most uncoordinated fucking I had ever done. But damn, it was good. Stuff that dreams were made of.

FLORINA

There wasn't anything nice about this man. He was rough and brash with all his actions. Another woman wouldn't have liked it. I wasn't another woman.

There were no breaks. No recovery to come down. He fucked me, then shoved his head between my legs and ate my pussy. The dirtiness of this man licking our mixed juices was borderline ruthless, and I came so hard that the walls of my uterus echoed the aftermath for hours to come.

Before the night was done, he flipped me on my belly, lifted my ass, and fucked me from behind. Then he popped me on top of him and made me ride him hard and fast. Made? *Who was I kidding?* I wasn't sure whose idea it was, but hot damn, was I loving it as much as he was.

My body ached and hummed in places I didn't know I had. This coming from a girl who was used to being on the run constantly. It was a good thing, though, because my physical condition was made to keep up with his marathon sex drive. My bladder, not so much. I flopped off him to make for the bathroom, and his hand locked around my ankle and yanked me back. "Where the fuck do you think you are going?" His voice alone, all gruff and hoarse, made me want to eat his cock. If not for my bladder screaming for release.

"Need to pee." I pushed his hand off, slid off the bed, and made my way to the bathroom, very aware that he was following me. I was a wild girl. Used to so much shit that normal girls weren't. Privacy was something I would have liked but never had. With this man, I didn't even care to have it anymore. He leaned against the doorframe, watching me pee with dark emotion in his eyes.

"You are mine," he muttered softly but sharp with intent.

I rolled my eyes to the ceiling, got up, and flushed. I wasn't anyone's. Unfortunately. No one ever wanted me enough for that. Not Tata. Not Mama. Not anyone. It didn't stop me from wanting to be his, even though I knew it was a sex-filled delusion of his. I swayed my hips, trotted to the shower, and turned it to full blast. I was using his amenities to the max before he kicked me out. Before I could step in, I was pushed in and jammed between the wall and him. His cock jerked between my legs, and his scruff hit my neck. His voice was warm and hard, and it pierced my heart. "Say it. Say you are fucking mine."

He lit a fever in me. It was hot and delusional and made me want things. Like want to hold on to him for eternity. God. I wanted to be his. More than anything. But he would tire of me and kick me out. I wasn't going to give in to a sex-induced delusion, was I? "Yours." I guess I was.

"You'll never leave me," he demanded.

"No."

"Always be home to welcome me."

"Yes."

He pushed his throbbing dick inside. "Always take my cock."

A ridiculous smile lit my face. "Yes."

"Only my cock." He bit my neck.

"Yes."

"No sucking off anyone else," he growled as his hands kept me pinned to the tiled wall.

"Only you."

He pulled out and pushed in. He did it again and again. The water and his balls slapped against me. My hands pushed against the tiles. His nails scraped on my back, drawing a pattern I couldn't keep track of. I was so close. Again. My legs trembled. Then he dropped his head next to my ear and said seven words that made me erupt. "I marked my name on your back."

This man was brutal. There wasn't anything nice in him. Yet his gestures flowed with kindness as natural as a stream in the midst of a forest. How could I ever deserve him?

CHAPTER EIGHT

FLORINA

There comes a time when a girl like me knows that good things aren't here to last. They never did. It had been two weeks. Two weeks of fucking every night like we were diseased, and fucking was the only way we could get it out of our blood. Two weeks of shared meals and washing up. Two weeks of intent stares and static vibes that electrified the molecules in my body into believing a lie.

Because this couldn't be anything but a lie. A delusion leaking into my blood and clouding my judgement. There was no way this could ever last.

He acted like I was his lifeline. The very air he needed to breathe. He touched me like I was precious. Came inside me like I was the only treasure he wanted in life. It was a lie. I was sure of it. No man so handsome, so good, could ever want me like he did.

This would end. If not today, then tomorrow. If not

tomorrow, then the next week. Only I was a woman who took control, and I was deciding to end it. Today.

The first step was to sneak out of the laundry room window at the back of the house. I was right. If I had really wanted to, I could have left this house the second he went upstairs that night two weeks ago.

Every day he left here, he told me with his deep, intense eyes fixed on me to stay inside. That was the only way he could protect me. Every day, I listened. Not today. *Who was I kidding?* No one had ever stood up for me. Step one to end this was done.

The easiest thing would have been to run through the trees to the darn hole I had cut out in the metal fence. But the masochist in me wanted him to see who I was. Who I really was. Before I left him for good.

I could have stayed. Hung around for a bit longer. But he had to be...him. He was so freaking nice it made me want to burst out in sobs. He should have known. I wasn't a woman born for nice things. I really wasn't.

With a heaviness that far outweighed the trudge of my muddy sneakers, I made my way to the villa. The house loomed ahead of the path, taunting me silently. *What are you doing, girl?* Taking back control. That's what I was doing. I was back in my old clothes, which taunted me about how much I must have stunk when I first met him. I had stood in front of his cupboard with my hands on another shirt of his with an ache to live in them as I'd done for the past two weeks. But why take a slow burn when you can jab a knife into my fucking heart? It was better to cut my losses. From everything once and for all.

Now, just a few minutes later, regret pooled in my heart. My hair and body were fresh from a shower, but the stink of my clothes put my gag reflex on edge. I had washed them three fucking times. Still, the smell clung to me as hard as the shambles of my life. This is what he had done. Two weeks and I couldn't stand the life I had been used to.

I ducked in between trees and bushes because I didn't want to be caught before I made it to the house. Crouching next to the bins, I peeped through the kitchen window, and my heart bolted to a stop. *Cristo.* Whipping around, I pasted my back to the wall, trying to calm my harsh breaths. I hadn't been around the house during the day, and the women in the kitchen were a sharp reminder of that. *I can do this.* I shouldn't have been doing this. But I couldn't stop myself if I had even wanted to.

Creeping under the windowsill, I edged my face closer and watched the scene before me. Watching other people's happy lives unfold before me was a pain I could have done without. A few maids were there, but my attention shot like a magnet to the brown woman carrying a child on her hip. She was the lady of the house. I could tell. The way she moved and spoke was so elegant. Something I would never be. My man... no, not my man. Marco could have clad me in gold, and I still wouldn't be like her. She was talking to a younger woman like she didn't have a care in the world. She didn't need to count the pennies in her pocket to match the distance that would get her away from here. She didn't need to wonder when the next time would be when she could find a warm bed. Instead, she smiled and tickled the baby on her hip.

The door leading to the inner part of the house swung open, and a small child flew through it, followed by an older woman. The brown lady laughed as the child hid under the table and the older woman pretended to look for her. The brightness of their lives was a glare in my face. The table where I had sat down and had my first meal with Marco was now clouded with bright wooden toys. They didn't even have the trash toys. They had the pretty ones. The ones sold in quaint little shops. This was the life Marco would one day have. He should have a wife like the brown lady. Not me, who didn't even know to eat like a nice lady.

I dropped down on my haunches. Nothing like seeing what I could never become to know I stood out here like horse shit on a clean floor. I should have just stepped inside that kitchen and got it over with. But I couldn't do it. Couldn't bring myself to be the lousy memory for those children.

They were so clean. So pretty. I would have tainted them with my smell. With my looks. So I sneaked around the corner and found an open door. It was a laundry room. If the fresh scent of lavender didn't give it away, the starched white shirts hanging on to a thin metal line did. The washing machines hummed quietly as I sneaked past and walked through a small hallway. The irony of it. These people didn't have one but three of these machines.

The laughter from the kitchen floated beneath the door and edged the outline of my heart. A yearning, deep and painful, took hold of me. Where you were born really did mark your life. If only I'd been born somewhere else. To different parents. Someone who loved me. I could have been in there with that beautiful brown woman. She would be nice to me, I was sure. But not this me. Never this me. I kept my burning eyes on my sneakers and made my feet move. *Get this over with, you stupid woman.*

I walked into an open hallway. It was big and rich. The first time I'd been in this house was a few years ago. Peppe had brought me in and taken me to the library. That room alone had been bigger than anything I'd lived in. He'd taken me through the back door, and I'd never passed this hallway. I would have remembered if I had. Warm white marble tiles on the floor, a crystal chandelier hanging from the ceiling, and a walnut wood banister curling around a spiral staircase. Quaint little furniture pieces were set against corners like someone had given it a lot of thought and had them made to measure because they fit perfectly. Like the glossy images of a mansion in a magazine. Only thing that repelled this perfect image was the sight of me.

Fuck. I wanted to be anywhere but here. But every time Marco fucked me, it felt like he cracked my heart. Now, it was lined with too many cracks, and I was terrified it would burst into a zillion pieces if he did it one more time. Then what would I have left? I was poor, but I at least owned my heart. What if he took that from me, too?

I didn't understand how he made me feel. He made me deranged. He made me mad. He made me careless and easy. The craziest thing was that I wanted to be whatever he wanted. Night and day.

I didn't want to be Florina the random Rromani girl. I wanted to be his. For once in my life, I wanted someone to want me like I was his and only his.

I wasn't sure if it was courage or stupidity, but something made me pull my way up along the pretty stairs. This part of the house was private, I could tell instantly. The floor told stories of children's feet running, little hands catching along the bannisters, and the walls spoke of clandestine meet-ups between their mamma and papa.

The first door I opened was like a fist to my heart. It was a nursery. All pretty, pink, and soft. *I should take something from here.* The Florina I knew would have done it. But I couldn't. My feet wouldn't budge beyond the threshold, and with a sigh, I closed the door softly and trudged a few doors further.

This one opened to the master bedroom. I knew it the moment the door swung open. The room spoke of passionate nights and special memories. All of them private. My feet hovered uncertainly. I didn't want to cross this line. A few heartbeats of hesitation, and I made myself do it, anyway. I stepped into the room, dirty sneakers and all.

Dark, charcoal walls and a warm wooden bed with ivory cotton sheets. A room to the left only for clothes, and a bathroom to the right so big I was sure it could house a king. And a queen. Because the numerous scented bottles lying around spoke of a woman's touch.

Last time I'd sneaked into this house, the Capizzi brothers had been single. Not anymore, I guessed. At least one of them was taken. I waited for the disappointment. Because in a distant past, I'd imagined seducing them, my ticket to a better life. But now, all I felt was the hurt that was yet to come when I showed Marco what I was capable of. My chipped nails ran over tiny bottles in pretty pink. I hadn't had my nails polished in ages. It looked expensive. Like one bottle could pay for an entire meal. Why I needed it, I didn't know. What was the point of pretty nails when your stomach was empty? But I chucked it into the pocket of my shabby dress anyway. *That should do it,* I convinced myself, even though, in my heart of hearts, I knew I should have taken more. And I almost made it out of the room without putting my grubby hands on their pretty things, except for the sparkle that beckoned to me from the small table next to the bed. A soft lamp and a half-burned candle sat on it.

But it was the pretty earrings that called out my name. I knew I shouldn't. Instinct told me this was going to be the worst betrayal of all. But when had it ever stopped me? Stepping towards the earrings, I grabbed them in my hand and squeezed them in between my palms. They were heavy, looked old and cherished. But they were gold and pretty. I opened my palm and looked at them again. It looked like an Asian design, and I knew they belonged to the pretty lady. Regret washed over me. I didn't want to hurt her. Indecision riled me. I might have put them back. I would never know. Because even as I was thinking of it, the mood changed like an impending storm and I just knew, even before I turned, that someone was onto me.

My breath choked in my throat. Antonio Capizzi

stood leaning against the door, hands fisted in his pockets with a jaw thumping loud enough to win over an elephant stampede.

"Who the fuck are you?" Even as the words flew towards me, I saw the recognition in his eyes. I shrank away from him, but it was too late. It was like I'd gone back a few years, and he'd caught me in the library. Stalking over to me, he yanked me by my arm and charged downstairs, pulling me with him.

A vase standing on a console at the bottom of the stairs crashed and shattered into a million pieces just before I hit the floor painfully, hitting my hip against the jagged edge of a table leg.

"Show me your fucking hands." His tone was quiet, lined with danger, and I was stupid, so I shrunk further from him. I had wanted to show Marco what I could do. So he would see that I wasn't worth it. I wasn't the one he imagined me to be. *Not this. Never this.* Girls who played with fire were sure to get burned one day. I guessed I would scatter into ashes today.

"Show me your fucking hands." This time, he roared so loud the cracked pieces of porcelain around me shrivelled further away. The joy from the kitchen stopped, followed by the soft patter of feet. The door swung open, and an "Antonio" floated through to the hallway.

Antonio Capizzi's face softened for a moment, and I mistakenly thought it was for me. But he ruffled his hand through his hair and muttered. "Not now, *mia cara*. Stay in the kitchen and keep the kids there."

I couldn't see her, but I knew she hadn't moved. He knew it, too, because he turned and imploded, "*Per favore, tesoro."* A heartbeat of silence, soft feet pattered away, and the kitchen door swung shut. *I guess she listened*. For some reason, I didn't want the pretty lady to see me like this.

She was so pretty, and she listened to her husband. I would, too, if someone said please and darling in one sentence. *But wasn't that what Marco did when he called me his la mia cocco?*

Guilt ate at my heart. It hurt more than the fear when Antonio Capizzi directed his gaze back to me. "Now open up those fucking hands."

My back was towards the table, and I caved half underneath it as he approached. Even when my wobbling hands opened to reveal the treasure I'd stolen, he didn't stop his stalking towards me. He halted a few feet away, but it was enough to put the fear of death into me. The second time I'd come close to it with him.

"Do you know how precious those earrings are to my wife?" he asked like I was an idiot not to know this. "Anything else you could have taken, and I wouldn't have cared. But you had to take this." He took a step further. "Drop them," he ordered, and I did it instantly because the tone in his voice commanded it. He leaned down, snatched them, and pocketed them with a tight look on his face. His movements were so elegant it was like watching a lion preying on its kill. "Now." He whipped a hand over his jaw. "What should I do with you?"

"Nothing." Marco's voice darted from behind him and shot right into my heart. *Shit.*

The silence in the hallway was so deadly it screamed like the aftermath of a war. The eeriness of disaster swirled in the room. Only the slight stiffness in Antonio Capizzi's shoulders gave away that he'd heard him.

My plan had been simple. Go into the house, steal something, throw it in Marco's face, piss him off, and get the hell out of here.

But I didn't foresee this. I thought I was smart. Turned out I wasn't even that. The little dignity that I had died when he walked into my line of sight. I couldn't bear to see the anger in his eyes. Mine burned hot with unshed tears. Suddenly, all I wanted to do was to go back to this morning. To how he was when he took me in the shower. He had looked like I was his heaven. But it was too late now. All because I had to go and ruin it.

I swallowed the bile in my throat and pulled my gaze to find the rage in his eyes. Instead, all I saw was pain. I might have preferred a bullet to my cracked heart than the look in his eyes. I was truly broken now.

"Come here, *la mia cocco.*" He offered his hand, but I refused to take it. I didn't understand. He had to be mad. Why wasn't he mad? With a sigh, he wrapped his hand around my wrist and pulled me off the floor. The laser beams prowling across me watched as Marco tucked me under his arm almost possessively. This must have been a dream. And a nightmare.

"So..." he drawled, a lazy tone to his voice, so different than his tone with me, "who is she?" He nodded towards me.

I don't know what I expected. But Marco saying, "My woman" wasn't it. I was more shocked than the man across from me because his eyes glinted with darkness, but there wasn't a shred of shock to be found in them.

"I knew a woman was the reason for your itchy attitude."

Marco stayed quiet. I shrunk further away and tried to hide behind him. He refused to let me and kept me pinned to his side like he was proud of me or something.

"You know she's—"

"I know." He didn't allow Antonio to finish his sentence. His tone was so full of defiance, as if he was on his feet, ready for a fight.

Antonio Capizzi's eyes followed us both like he was watching two specimens under his microscopic eyes. "She fucking took Divya's earrings."

"I know."

"You going to keep her in line?"

Marco stiffened next to me. "I am giving you my word."

I looked at the man next to me with a thump in my heart. Why would he do that? He knew he couldn't control me. But he gave his word to the *consigliere* of the *Cosa Nostra*. He wouldn't be able to keep it.

But Antonio Capizzi seemed to think he would. "Don't make me fucking regret it, Marco." With that, he swung past us and walked towards the kitchen.

CHAPTER NINE

MARCO

I couldn't pull her fast enough from the house. Couldn't hide her deep enough, away from dangerous men. Antonio was a lot of things, but he kept his word. His men, I didn't trust. I couldn't.

They take one look at this woman sneaking around the house yelling for trouble, there'd be a crimson hole where her heart was before I could even think of reaching for my gun. Which was fucking why I'd told her to stay inside the house.

Fuck! These feelings. I hated it. It was like watching my heart go for a ride on the highway, leaving me behind. Anger coursed through me for putting herself in this position. The sight of her half under the table, amidst broken pieces of a fucking vase and Antonio with murder in his eyes and a gun within reach, had been enough to take ages off my life.

I'd been surprised I hadn't keeled over and died.

Instead, I had stood up to him and tested a lifelong friendship. It was high fucking time I started praying because the man above must have put me in his good books.

My nails dug into her wrist as I pulled her along the gravelly path. I had half a mind to shove her onto the ground and whip her ass right here out in the open air. Did she have a fucking death wish? What the fuck was she thinking? My breath came out in gasps, and by the time the front door flew open in my house, I'd worked myself up for a fucking war.

I pulled her through the hall and pushed her into the living room. The front door banged shut, creaking angrily on its hinges. This woman was one day going to cost me a house, and then we'd fucking both be homeless.

Safely inside, I let my anger roll. "What the fuck were you thinking?"

She glared at me with murder in her eyes. What the fuck was she angry for? Rage gushed inside my body like blood spurting from a bust vein. She couldn't have felt it because she made to move away, and I shoved my feet to block her. "Talk. Now."

"It was going to happen, anyway."

I shook my head, trying to clear my thoughts. *What did I fucking miss?* "What's going to happen?"

"You were going to throw me out," she huffed, her shoulders stiff, arms crossed.

Again. What did I fucking miss? "When did I say that?"

"You didn't, but you were going to, anyway."

"Don't you dare put fucking words in my mouth. Why would I even do that?"

"Because you'll tire of me!" Her words darted across the room, hit the hard planes of each wall, and shot right into my heart. Her pain was so evident it was tangible, like a thick concrete barricade circling around her. My anger sputtered and ebbed.

"Why would I do that, *la mia cocco*?" I asked her softly.

She blinked and squeezed her hands tightly to her stomach. "You tell me."

I stared at the woman in front of me. She tried to hide behind filthy clothes, but her warm heart was custom-made for me, like one of those fine suits Antonio loved. She was the fucking heat to my cold nights and the comfort to my lost days. Couldn't she see she was the one?

She took a step back and frowned at the look on my face. A nervous laugh bounced off her and echoed in the silent room. "What?" She shuffled with her feet. "You love me or something?"

"Or something," I said roughly. I stepped towards her, and she backed away.

"No." She shook her head.

"You can't tell me how to feel, *la mia cocco*."

"Stop calling me your fucking coconut." One step back, and I moved one forward. "I am not your fucking anything."

"You are my fucking everything."

"No. No. No." Her fisted hands dropped to her sides.

"Yes. Yes. Yes," I whispered softly.

Another step back, and she pleaded with her big brown eyes. "Just let me go."

"Never." I crowded her and walked her towards the wall. Before her next breath, I'd shed her frumpy clothes and shoved her face first towards the rough wall. I pushed my mouth near her ear and muttered angrily, "I'll never let you leave. Don't you remember? You promised the first day we fucked that you'll never leave."

Her shoulders shook with tears, and her voice whimpered, "I don't deserve you."

My hands trembled as I unzipped and pulled my dick out. Emotion crowded my throat. "Oh, *la mia cocco,* I am the one who doesn't deserve you. The only reason for you to leave is if I am unworthy." My hands clenched around her ass as I rubbed my face on her neck. "Do you think I am unworthy of you?" I asked, even though the juvenile in me just wanted to demand that she stay.

"No," she yelled brokenly, and relief fuelled my heart.

"Then promise me you'll stay."

She groaned as I pushed my cock inside her juicy pussy. "Shut up and say the words," I demanded, even though my words made little sense.

"I promise," she sniffled, and I knew I had her.

I shuffled the dirty clothes off her angrily until she was fully naked, rid of her old life. She was now just the way I liked her. Pure. Her perfect ass pasted to me, my cock throbbing inside her.

I pulled out and pounded into her. "No more stealing, Rina. You understand? I am not risking your life again." Just the thought of it made me angry, and I whacked her ass hard to let her know. She jerked forward and moaned loudly like she loved it. Of course she would. Custom-made for me, this one. "Understand? You want something, you ask me. *Sì?*"

"*Sì. Sì.*"

Yes. She loosened the last shred of control I had, and I pounded into her. We drove ourselves mad as we always did and went at it like wild beasts. When we came, we were loud, and we were messy, but I wouldn't have it any other way. My own woman. My fucking family.

All my life, I'd wanted to be a part of something. Like a broken puzzle, I'd rolled through life looking for the missing piece. Turned out this glorious woman in front of me was it. We came together with our broken souls and made them whole. *Fuck.* We weren't perfect. But we were us. That was enough for me.

EPILOGUE

TWO MONTHS LATER.

FLORINA

The TV blasted Romanian. Marco had arranged for all Romanian channels to be set up on our TV and poisoned me with my new addiction. Romanian soap operas. I lifted myself off the couch I'd been lounging on and strolled lazily to the kitchen. Being lazy was my new activity these days. After all, what was a girl to do if she didn't have to hunt for a roof to sleep under or look for a meal to eat? So, my days were filled with watching TV, napping, and cooking. Just so I wouldn't feel too entitled and call myself a rich white woman, I threw in some Italian and English lessons. I'd been quick to pick up languages everywhere I went. It turned out I had a talent for it. Imagine that. Me having a talent for anything other than to suck strange men's cocks. I'd given up on that talent now. The only cock in my mouth these days had a direct link to my heart.

I took the pot from the drawer next to the cooker

and set it on the burner. I was in the mood for some curry. The pretty brown lady...*cristo*...I need to stop calling her that. Divya, as she had requested I call her, had shown me how to make one, and even though I'd made it two days ago, I was in the mood for one again. Something about the burn from the spices sliding down my throat made it addictive. Just like my soap operas.

I was right. Divya was nice to me. She truly didn't seem to care where I was from. Her husband, not so much. He didn't say or do anything to make me feel out of place, but his glares told me he hadn't forgiven me yet. I'd been annoyed. Until I learned that those earrings had been a gift from Divya's dead dad to her dead mum. Yeah, I wouldn't forgive myself, either.

I was reaching for the garam masala on the top shelf when warm hands squeezed my naked ass. I flicked a glance behind my shoulder. *How did I end up winning this man?* He stood behind me with nothing but a towel around his hips and a devilish grin on his thick lips. I swatted his hands off me. "I'm going to cook."

He ignored me and let his hands bunch his shirt I was wearing and roll it onto my back.

"Marco," I whined half-heartedly.

When his harsh voice vibrated in my ear, I abandoned my plans for cooking. "Dessert first."

Fuck, this man. He was hot and horny all the time, and I wasn't complaining. The garam masala stayed in the cupboard. I reached back and tugged his towel, and it dropped in a thick heap on the floor. His hands made work of popping my buttons and swept inside to squeeze my tits.

"Had a good day?" he asked right before he plunged two fingers inside me.

I groaned loudly.

"Hmm..." he urged.

"Did nothing." The night was dark, and I caught our reflection staring back at us from the window. Fuck, we looked hot.

"Fucking perfect," he growled, biting my shoulder with his eyes on our reflection.

I wasn't sure if he meant perfect that I did nothing, or that I was perfect. Knowing him, he meant both.

"I need to earn my living—"

A sharp whack stung my ass, and his fingers pulled out. "You are." He plunged his cock in. "By taking my cock."

I rolled my eyes. He'd taken to calling me his custom-made whore since he'd found my kink for dirty name calling. He was still as I fell with my forearms on the countertop and shoved my ass back. It was crazy shit talk for anyone but us. For us, this was what worked. He pulled out and said with a devious gleam in his eyes, "I had a great day today."

I scowled. His days were made up of beating up and killing men. "Who did you kill?"

"No one."

"So what did—"

"I bought you something." His hand stroked my ass with something hard and cold and tiny. It moved from the cleft of my butt, up my back to my shoulder, and rode down my left arm. I watched his big-fisted hands, clearly hiding something from my prying eyes. One pulse point and something glided over my fingers, and my breath halted. There was a dull gold line on my finger.

"You're marrying me."

In typical Marco style, he didn't ask. Emotion clogged my throat at the sight of my finger. It was dull gold and had a small, intricate pattern that looked Indian. That was Marco's style, too. He knew that I truly loved those earrings.

"Did Divya help you choose?" I couldn't bring my gaze away from the gold on my finger. It didn't even sparkle. It was dull gold, like an ancient piece of jewellery that had led inside a cave for centuries, and I loved it so much.

"Fuck yes. The only good taste I had was spent when I chose you. Say yes."

I pulled my eyes off it to meet his in the reflection.

"It wasn't a question."

"Fuck no." He gave me an angry stare before he plunged in again, pulling a loud moan from me. "You are mine."

"Yes," I whispered, even if he hadn't waited for a yes.

He worked us both, pumping in and out. Our eyes were glued to each other in the mirror. I lifted myself up and pasted my back to his front. His big hand was rough and pinched my nipples painfully. Shots of pleasure swept through my body. His other hand came to the front. I watched in the mirror as it glided down and pinched my clit. The pride on his face as he watched me was what dreams were made of.

Some women would want their man to be on his knee and ask. But my man, he did it butt naked while he was vulnerable and inside me. I guessed love was different for everyone.

His cock stroked my magic spot, and my world burst into a million pieces. He pumped harsh and deep like a lunatic, and my muscles squeezed all his cum out. I fell on my forearms to the worktop, and he landed on top of me. He was sweaty and heavy. Just the way I liked it.

My love was different.

My love was him. Pure and naked.

My love was him killing an Albanian for me.

My love was him defending me.

My love was him not judging me for my past.

My love was him. Him. Him.

I'd take the whole world on if I had him by my side.

WANT to know more about Antonio and Divya?

Read all about them and how Florina got caught in the library in Nanny to the Mafia.

ALSO BY SOPHIA RAZ

The Shadows of Cosa Nostra Chronicles:

Did you love Lorenzo and Daria?

Curious to know more about Antonio and Divya?
Read the other books from The Shadows of Cosa Nostra Chronicles by scanning the QR code below.

The Shadows of Cosa Nostra Chronciles:

Nanny to the Mafia:

Book 01 - Antonio and Divya's story

Princess of the Mafia:

Book 02 - Lorenzo and Daria's story

Runaway in the Mafia:

Book 03 - Vitale and Ahana's story

Book 04 - Pre-order now

The Shadows of Cosa Nostra Chronicles - Novellas:

Hustler in the Mafia:

Novella 01.5 - Marco and Florina's story

AFTERWORD

Shhh...

Do you hear that music in the background?
That's me doing a little jingle because you took a chance on my writing and read my book.
Thank you for your time and your trust.

If you enjoyed my book nothing would make me happier than a review. If you could just help one reader find their way to a new book, that's one story being read.
I would appreciate you leaving a review.

ABOUT THE AUTHOR

Sophia met her forbidden MMC and crossed continents for love. She was born and raised in South-East Asia and now lives in Europe with him and their daughter. Sophia's own love story inspired her to rediscover her passion for writing.

She writes about love beyond cultural and racial boundaries. A defiance of what is 'expected' in favour of what is right. Her strong-willed, unapologetic, principled FMCs don't settle for less than they deserve, even if it means breaking social convention or cultural rules. Sophia's MMCs, while being jealous, possessive heroes, will place the heroine at the centre of their world and are willing to change and learn to gain trust and respect.

When Sophia is not writing, she's busy being an entrepreneur or enjoying quality time with her family. Aside from that, she loves to have an authentic connection with her readers, so feel free to reach out to Sophia.